The Terrible Underpants

*Real hairy-nosed wombats don't live with little girls, they live
in the bush. If you would like to help wombats such as the threatened
Northern Hairy-nosed Wombat, you can help try to protect the places
where wombats need to live. World Wide Fund for Nature Australia
Threatened Species Network, GPO Box 528, Sydney, NSW 2001.
The Australian Conservation Foundation Land Clearing Campaign,
340 Gore Street, Fitzroy, Victoria 3065.*

Puffin Books
Penguin Books Australia Ltd
250 Camberwell Road, Camberwell, Victoria 3124, Australia
Penguin Books Ltd
80 Strand, London WC2 0RL, England
Penguin Putnam Inc.
375 Hudson Street, New York, New York 10014, USA
Penguin Books Canada Limited
10 Alcorn Avenue, Toronto, Ontario, Canada M4V 3B2
Penguin Books (NZ) Ltd
Cnr Rosedale and Airborne Roads, Albany, Auckland, New Zealand
Penguin Books (South Africa) (Pty) Ltd
24 Sturdee Avenue, Rosebank, Johannesburg 2196, South Africa
Penguin Books India (P) Ltd
11, Community Centre, Panchsheel Park, New Delhi 110 017, India

First published by Penguin Books Australia Ltd 2000
First Published in Picture Puffin 2001

3 5 7 9 10 8 6 4 2

Designed by Tony Palmer, Penguin Design Studio
Typeset in 22 pt Cochin
Printed and bound by South China Printing Co. Hong Kong, China

National Library of Australia
Cataloguing-in-Publication data:

Cooke, Kaz, 1962–.
The terrible underpants.

ISBN 0 140 56882 4.

I. Title.

A823.3

www.penguin.com.au

THE TERRIBLE UNDERPANTS

Written and Illustrated by

Kaz Cooke

PUFFIN BOOKS

My name is Wanda-Linda,
and this is Glenda.
She is a hairy-nosed wombat.

'Wanda-Linda and Glenda!'
my dad called out one morning.
'It's time to get dressed.'

(Actually, because Glenda is
a hairy-nosed wombat,
she hardly ever gets dressed.)

I put on a dress,
but I couldn't find any underpants.

'Mum,' I said, 'where are all my underpants?'

'Ask your dad,' Mum said.

'Dad,' I said, 'where are all my underpants?'

'Ask your mum,' Dad said.

'Um. Are they in the washing machine?'
Mum asked.

'NO!' I said.

'Did I hang them on the line?'
Dad called out.

'YES!' I yelled back.

'You can't wear wet unders,' Mum said.

'How about these?'

OH NO!

NOT THE TERRIBLE UNDERPANTS!

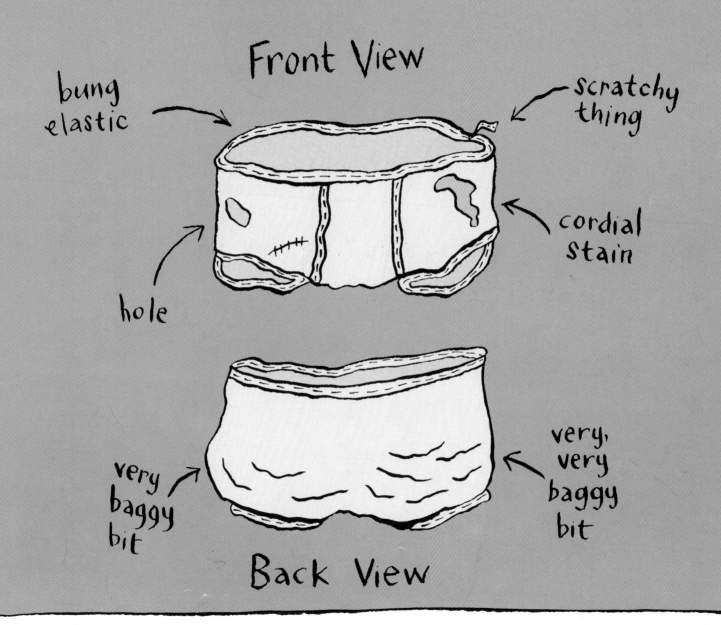

I wish I had a pair of
Perfectly Marvellous Underpants instead.

lovely and comfy
good elastic
moon and stars
leg hole
other leg hole

'Never mind,' said Dad.
'Nobody will notice The Terrible Underpants.'

'Quite frankly,' I replied,
'I find that very difficult to believe.'

We went to the shop, and a dirty big wind
blew up my dress.
Mrs Kafoops from down the street saw
The Terrible Underpants.

'My giddy aunt, Wanda-Linda,' she said.
'What a frightful pair of underpants.'

Later I played upside down on the monkey bars,
and all the other kids saw
The Terrible Underpants.

Glenda was appalled.

When I got home I ran through
the sprinkler to cool down,
and Mum said, 'Those really are
Terrible Underpants, Wanda-Linda.'

'I KNOW!' I said.

I did a handstand,
and somebody in a helicopter took a picture
and put it on the TV.
And EVERYBODY in the WHOLE WORLD saw
The Terrible Underpants.

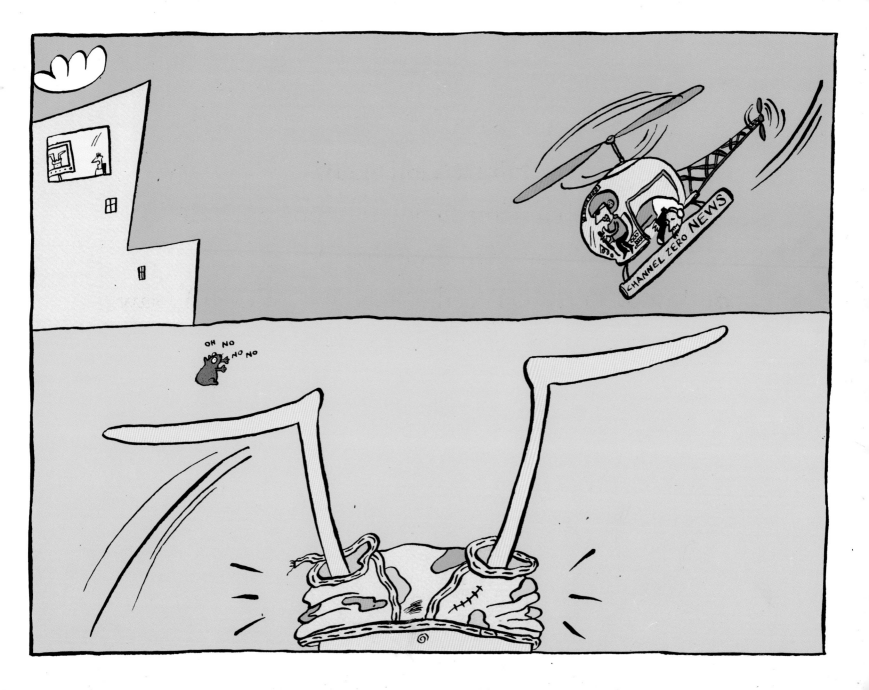

So I took them off.

THE END